ORION
&
THE ORCAS

BY

DEBBIE BAILEY

ISBN: 1494271788

ISBN-13: 9781494271787

Library of Congress Control Number: 2014903187

CreateSpace Independent Publishing Platform

North Charleston, South Carolina

For:

Maureen

Illustrations by Denis Proulx

CHAPTER ONE

Orion was really looking forward to her family's weekend fishing trip. Her dad, mom, and big brother Travis had been talking about nothing else since her father surprised them all with a brand new boat on Tuesday. Her family lived in a house right on the beach in San Diego, and Orion would look out at the ocean and daydream about catching more fish than anyone else.

When Saturday came, Orion's family and their friends, another family of four, all put on their lifejackets and headed out to sea. Once they were about a mile away from the beach, Orion's dad stopped the engine. The parents got out their fishing poles. Travis and his best friend, Cameron, got out poles too, but not the girls. Orion's friend, Christy, didn't want to fish, but Orion wanted to very much.

"Please dad," she said, "Let me fish with you."

Her brother Travis said, "You can't catch a fish. You're too little."

"I'm not too little," said Orion. "I'm eight!"

Her dad said, "Honey, you are too little for sea fishing, but next time we'll go to a lake, and I'll set you up with your own little pole.....alright?"

"Ok, Dad," she said.

All afternoon, she watched her parents catch fish. She watched their friends catch fish, and she watched her brother catch fish.

Everyone was having a wonderful time....except Orion.

"I'm so tired of being told that I'm too little for this, or too young for that," thought Orion.

"I'm NOT too little to catch a fish!" she said out loud. "I'm gonna catch one, and surprise all of them!"

She grabbed the smallest fishing pole she could find, and went to the back of the boat all alone. She tried to put the hook in the water to catch a fish, but the pole was too big for her to handle. Orion dropped the fishing pole, and it fell and hung up on top of the boat engine.

"OH NO!" she cried. "I'm in BIG trouble, now!"

Just as she leaned over to reach the pole, her dad started up the boat to go back home. Orion and the fishing pole both went flying into the water! No one heard her calls for help, because the boat engine was too loud. Even though she was afraid, Orion started swimming as fast as she could, but it was no use. She couldn't catch up with her family's boat.

Orion became so tired from swimming, she stopped. In fact, she fell asleep, but was kept above water by the lifejacket. It was only when her family was almost home, they realized she was missing! Her dad turned the boat around to find her, but it was too late. While she was sleeping, a large black shape had come up beneath her, and carried Orion away!

CHAPTER TWO

Orion woke up the next morning, but she was not in her bed. She was on the back of an orca whale! She was surrounded by the open sea, and five orcas! At first, she was scared, but the baby orca rubbed up against her leg and made sweet sounds to her. Orion knew the baby was trying to make friends.

She slid off the big orca's back and into the water. Orion and the baby orca swam and played together. After a while, Orion started feeling thirsty and hungry. She couldn't swallow fish like the orca whales did...YUCK! But she watched the baby orca feed, and get milk from her mom.

When the baby orca was done, she wondered if the mom would let her milk her like a cow. "But what will I put the milk in?" Orion asked herself.

She saw some kelp, and swam over to it. She broke off one of the bulbs, and then swam over to the mom pushing on her, saying, "Mommy orca, I'm hungry! Please roll over on your back so I can milk you."

AND SHE DID!

Orion climbed on top of the mommy orca's tummy, and tugged on her until the milk filled up the bulb. The milk was warm and good. But the milk wasn't just warm, and the milk wasn't just good. After a few minutes, Orion started to feel different, and her skin started to look different too.

All the little wrinkles on her hands and feet from being in the sea went away, and Orion began to feel super strong. She ripped off the life jacket, undressed down to her bathing suit, and jumped off the mommy orca's tummy. She didn't know why, but Orion was swimming in the sea as quick as a fish!

"This is great!" she said. Then Orion heard someone answer back.

"Yeah, swimming fast is fun."

Orion turned, and saw it was the baby orca.

"You understood what I just said?" she asked.

"Sure! Human talk is easy for me to understand." said the baby.

"I can't believe it! Then she asked, "What's your name?"

"My name is Letty," said the baby orca.

"I'm Orion," replied the little girl. "Letty, can I talk to all the other whales?"

"Oh, no." said Letty. "I can't even understand my family yet. Only some of their sounds and clicks make sense to me."

"Well, how come we can talk to each other?" asked Orion.

"I don't know," said Letty. "Maybe because I'm brand new, or maybe because of the milk from my momma."

"Letty, what's your mom's name?" she asked.

"My momma's name is Chanee," said Letty, "and my poppa is Nimza. He's the one who saved you. The leader of our family is Quidera.

She's the one who said it was alright for my poppa to go get you. There's also Lizaron; she's Quidera's sister."

After thanking Nimza and Chanee for saving her and feeding her, Orion turned to her new friend and said, "Letty, let's see what else I can do."

Orion could swim fast with the whales! She could dive deep with the whales! She could jump high out of the water like a whale, and she came up laughing with joy. She was so excited and happy, but not everyone in the orca family was as pleased.

"This human child is going to cause problems for us," clicked Lizaron.

"We all know how you feel about humans, Lizaron," sounded back Quidera, "but the child is safe in our care, and you will not make trouble for her. Do you understand?"

"Yes, sister."

CHAPTER THREE

Orion loved being with the orcas, and they took such good care of her. In the morning, she used the kelp bulbs to drink the milk from. In the late afternoon, Orion would wrap some kelp up Nimza's fin to dry it out, and that would keep her warm while she slept on his back at night.

When the orcas went to hunt for food, Orion was always left behind with one of the grown-up whales. All the adult whales knew Orion was too young to understand, and that a hunt might scare the little girl.

To Orion, her days with the orcas were very special. Every morning, she watched the family of orcas play. They dove deep down in the sea playing chasing games. They slapped and sprayed water at each other. They even grabbed at each other's tails, pulling one another around, but Orion was too small and light to be a part of these games.

So, Letty and Chanee made up a game of their own for her. The mommy orca would hold her breath, and roll over. Orion would crawl up, and stand on her tail. Chanee would then give her tail a little flip, and Orion would go flying into the air! Once she dove into the sea, Letty would be there waiting for her. Then she would put her arms around Letty, and they would come straight up out of the water together. All three of them loved their game, and Orion began to feel a part of this close and loving family of whales.

CHAPTER FOUR

One morning after their game, Orion talked Letty into going off to explore together. They saw all kinds of beautiful and brightly colored sea flowers. They saw lots of pretty fish, and even a band of sea horses. Then Orion got an idea.

"Hey, Letty," she said, "Lets race."

"What?"

Orion replied, "Let's see who can swim the fastest."

Letty laughed and said, "You can't swim faster than a whale!"

"We'll see," Orion said, and asked, "Are you ready?"

"Yup, I'm ready." said the baby.

"When I say three, we go....Ok?" said Orion.

Letty said, " Ok....THREE!"

Then they both took off! They were swimming really fast with Letty in front by just an inch or two. Suddenly, they both stopped. Up ahead, they saw a shark.

After quickly coming up for air, Orion screamed, "A shark! It's a shark!"

"Yeah," replied Letty, "And sharks bite REALLY hard!"

Thankfully, Letty's poppa and momma heard their cries for help, and arrived just in time. Nimza rammed into the shark from one side, and Chanee rammed into the shark from the other. They spun that shark around in circles so fast that when it finally stopped spinning, it swam away as fast as it could!

That evening, Quidera sounded out, "I am becoming afraid for Orion's safety."

Chanee sounded back, "My baby loves her. I know we can work this out."

But Nimza agreed with Quidera.

"My love," clicked Nimza, "Orion must go home to her own world. She is from the world of land. She is not from the world of water."

Chanee sounded, "But where is her home? Where is her land place?"

Quidera decided to think about Orion some more.

CHAPTER FIVE

The next day, Orion saw pretty waves rising in the ocean.

"Letty, will you let me ride you on the waves?" she asked.

"Sure. Let's go!" replied the baby whale.

What they didn't know was that these waves were not to be played with.

Chanee sounded out to her baby, "A big storm is ahead, and Orion is in danger."

"Orion!" yelled Letty, "you have to get on Quidera's back right now!"

"What's wrong?" asked Orion.

She turned around, and saw a HUGE wave coming right at her! Quidera rose out of the sea, and Orion climbed onto her back and hung onto her fin. Quidera rode out the entire storm with Orion on her back, and kept her safe.

After the storm, Lizaron clicked out, "I told you she would be trouble."

Chanee sounded back. "Lizaron, she is not one of us. She just does not know how we do things."

At the same time, Orion and Letty were talking about the storm, too.

"The storm was very scary, Letty," said Orion, "but I love being here with all of you."

"I know, but we were so afraid for you." said Letty, and asked. "Orion, don't you miss your home and family?"

"I miss my family a lot." replied Orion. "But all the things I can do now....no other kid I know can do them. All the different fish, animals, and colors of the sea are so beautiful. The stars and the moon at night are so bright and magical. This is the greatest thing that's ever happened to me in my whole life!"

Letty laughed, and said, "Yeah, it's the greatest thing that's happened in my whole life, too!"

CHAPTER SIX

A couple of days later, Orion was sitting on Chanee's back, and resting up against her fin after breakfast. Out in the distance, she saw a school of dolphins. She jumped into the sea, and swam as fast as she could to catch up with them. When she got there, she tried to make friends with them, but Chanee and Letty were right behind her. When the dolphins saw the orca whales, they quickly rode away.

Letty said, "Come on back with us, Orion."

"What's the matter?" asked the little girl.

"Nothing's the matter. It's just that we always stay close together....especially the babies. It's for our safety."

"I'm sorry." she replied. "I didn't know."

"We understand that," said the baby orca. "I didn't even know until we got in trouble with that shark......remember?"

Orion nodded her head yes, and Letty said, "Don't feel bad. Come on, everything's alright."

Before they went to sleep that night, Orion had something to admit to Letty.

"I guess that's what my dad and my big meanie brother were trying to tell me."

"What are you talking about?" asked Letty.

"How do you think I got here? My dad and my brother were both trying to tell me that I'm too little to fish, but I didn't listen. I went off by myself without telling anyone, and that's how I fell off the boat. If Nimza hadn't saved me, what would have happened to me?"

"We'll never know that," said Letty. "But my poppa did save you, and it all worked out. Didn't it?"

Orion smiled and said, "Yeah, it did."

"Good!" said Letty. "I'll see you in the morning."

Meanwhile, Lizaron sounded to Quidera, "Orcas and dolphins are not enemies, but we certainly do not play together. She does not belong with us."

"Sister, Orion could be taught over time." clicked back Quidera. "That does not bother me. What bothers me is something else.

As we swim further north to our home by the land of ice, it won't matter how much Orion drinks. She won't be able to get enough fat from Chanee's milk to keep her warm, or keep her skin plump, or have even enough energy to keep up with us as we swim. Orion is not built like us."

"Agreed." sounded Lizaron, and then added, "Even I don't want harm to come to the child of land."

"Oh, Lizaron," sounded the leader of the family, "I know you don't want her with us, but something must be done, and soon."

CHAPTER SEVEN

The next day, Quidera made her decision. "We must go back. We must try to find Orion's land place."

"This will be hard for me." Chanee sounded sadly. "I love her like my own baby."

Letty was the only Orca that could tell Orion, and Nimza told her what the family had planned to do.

"I don't want Orion to go home!" sounded Letty as loud as she could, and then slapping her tail on the water added, "I want her to stay with us!"

"Do you want to see her get so cold that she stops speaking and moving?" clicked Nimza.

"No." clicked Letty quickly.

"Then we must take her home."

"OK, Poppa. I understand, and I'll tell her."

That evening, Orion was sitting on Nimza's back watching a ton of shooting stars in the sky.

"This is awesome!" she said out loud, "It's like having a fireworks show all to myself. It's so wonderful here."

Letty popped her head out of the water, "Yup, our world IS wonderful, but haven't you noticed that it's getting colder?"

 "Yeah." she said, and then asked. "Is it because we are so far out at sea?"

"No." said Letty, "It's because we are going home. We come to warm water once a year, but only for a short time. Our home is far away in cold icy water. Orion, you can't come with us."

"Don't say that," cried the little girl. "What do you mean?"

Letty told her friend, "We are turning around to take you home."

She jumped into the water, and held onto the baby orca saying, "Letty, I don't want to leave you!"

Letty replied, "I don't want you to leave me either, but there isn't anything else we can do. If you swim with us any further, you'll be hurt by the freezing ice water.

Orion sobbed, "I always knew I couldn't stay with you forever, but I didn't think it would end so soon."

CHAPTER EIGHT

Three days later, just before the sun came up, Orion and the orcas were back in the warm water of San Diego. Nimza and Letty swam close to shore with Orion, but the rest of the orcas stayed out at sea. LIzaron tried sounding to Chanee that they were doing the right thing for the little girl. The mommy orca knew it was true, but also knew how much she would miss Orion, and sprayed a bunch of water right in Lizaron's face!

Orion stood up on Nimza's back to see the land better.

After a while, she yelled out, "There's my home! There's my beach!"

Nimza carried her on the tip of his nose and headed for shore with Letty following beside them. Nimza gave her a soft nudge up to shallow water.

Orion turned around and looked at both of them.

She rubbed the poppa orca on his nose, saying, "Nimza, thank you for bringing me home. Thank you for everything."

Then she went to Letty. "I love you Letty." she said. "You're the best friend I've ever had." Then she hugged and kissed her friend goodbye.

"I love you, too, Orion." said Letty. And before the little girl let go of the little whale, the baby orca stuck out her tongue and licked Orion right on the face!

Nimza and Letty used the next wave to turn around and go back out to sea. When they reached the rest of the family, all five orcas raised their tails out of the ocean and waved goodbye to her. After waving back, she sat down on the beach and cried. Orion would miss her orca family very much.

Orion's mom was in the kitchen making the morning coffee. When she looked out the window, she couldn't believe her eyes. There, sitting in the sand, was her missing daughter! She ran out of the house and down the beach as fast as she could.

"Orion! Orion!" she yelled.

The little girl looked up and saw her mom. She got up on her feet, and they ran into each other's arms.

"Where have you been?" asked her mom with happy tears running down her cheeks. "What happened to you?"

"Mom, don't cry," said Orion, "I just went on a fishing trip of my own!"

Orion really was happy to be home, and her family was thrilled to see her. They hadn't stopped looking for her, and having her back was like a miracle. That evening at dinner, she told them all her stories about the orca whales. Her family didn't know what to believe, but it didn't matter. Orion was home.

"And, Dad, don't worry," she said, "you'll never have to tell me that I'm too little to do anything ever again."

Her dad chuckled knowing how curious his daughter is, and said, "Alright Honey, but I think we might be having this talk again sooner than you think."

As Orion got ready for bed that night, she remembered what Letty said. Every year this family of orca whales comes back to the warm San Diego water. She and Letty can be together again! Safe and sound with her family, Orion slept with sweet dreams of all the fun, friendship, and adventures to come between:

ORION & THE ORCAS

Dear Jackie,

Keep

Dreaming!

Love,

Debbie

Riley

44938747R00034

Made in the USA
Charleston, SC
05 August 2015